THE FIRST Christmas NIGHT

THE FIRST
Christmas
NIGHT

Written by Keith Christopher

Illustrated by Christine Kornacki

Worthy kids
ideals
Nashville, Tennessee

ISBN-13: 978-0-8249-5653-0

Published by Worthy Kids/Ideals
An Imprint of Worthy Publishing Group
A division of Worthy Media, Inc.
Nashville, Tennessee

Design by Georgina Chidlow

Color separations by Precision Color Graphics,
Franklin, Wisconsin
Printed and bound in China

Leo_Apr17_8

Library of Congress Cataloging-in-Publication Data
Christopher, Keith.
 The first Christmas night / written by Keith Christopher ;
illustrated by Christine Kornacki.
   pages cm
ISBN 978-0-8249-5653-0 (hard cover : alk. paper) 1. Jesus Christ—
       Nativity—Juvenile literature. I. Kornacki, Christine. II. Title.
BT315.3.C54 2013
232.92—dc23
                      2013012425

For Tammy, Kadie, and Nelson. —K.C.

To my mentors Dennis, Bill, Doug,
and Jeremiah. —C.K.

For unto us a child is born, unto us a son is given. . . .

—ISAIAH 9:6

'Twas the very first Christmas,
when all through the town
not a creature was stirring—
there was not a sound.

The moon, shining bright
in the heavens so high,
gave the luster of midday
to the Bethlehem sky.

The animals were nestled
in warm, cozy places,
with looks of contentment
on each of their faces.

And Mary and Joseph,
   so tired from the road,
had just settled in to
   a humble abode.

To a Bethlehem stable
they had traveled with care.
They knew that their baby
soon would be there.

And then, in the stable,
a baby's first cry!
Peace on earth, good will—
redemption is nigh.

He had not a crib,
    but in a manger instead,
the tiny new baby
    lay down his sweet head.

Mary looked down at
his cute little nose
and silently counted—
ten fingers, ten toes.

As shepherds kept watch
on a small, nearby hill,
their sheep were all silent
and sleepy and still.

When suddenly in the sky
there arose such a sight—
one angel, then many,
appeared in the night.

The heavens rejoiced
  as their story unfurled:
a baby, a Savior,
  had been born to the world.

So the shepherds arose
to search for the place
to get a close look at the
baby's sweet face.

Then, out of the East,
there came royalty
whose mission was finding
the Savior, you see.

When they finally found
the babe they had sought,
gold, frankincense, and myrrh
were the gifts that they brought.

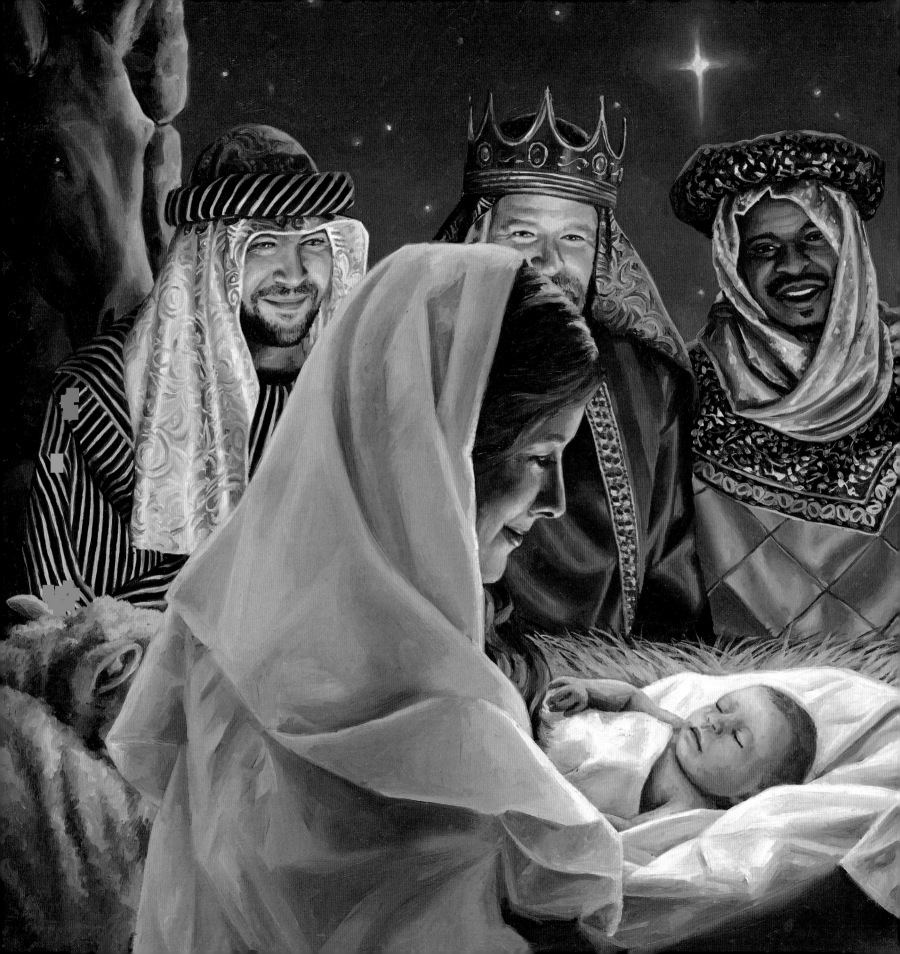

So the wise men bowed down
and praised his sweet name.
Soon all those who heard
would rejoice that he came.

And now we that know
can say with delight,

The Biblical Story of the First Christmas

And it came to pass in those days, that there went out a decree from Caesar Augustus that all the world should be taxed. . . . And Joseph also went up from Galilee, out of the city of Nazareth, into Judaea, unto the city of David, which is called Bethlehem; . . . To be taxed with Mary his espoused wife, being great with child. And so it was, that, while they were there, the days were accomplished that she should be delivered. And she brought forth her firstborn son, and wrapped him in swaddling clothes, and laid him in a manger; because there was no room for them in the inn.

And there were in the same country shepherds abiding in the field, keeping watch over their flock by night. And, lo, the angel of the Lord came upon them, and the glory of the Lord shone round about them: and they were sore afraid. And the angel said unto them, Fear not: for, behold, I bring you good tidings of great joy, which shall be to all people. For unto you is born this day in the city of David a Saviour, which is Christ the Lord. And this shall be a sign unto you; Ye shall find the babe wrapped in swaddling clothes, lying in a manger. And suddenly there was with the angel a multitude of the heavenly host praising God, and saying, Glory to God in the highest, and on earth peace, good will toward men. And it came to pass, as the angels were gone away from them into heaven, the shepherds said one to another, Let us now go even unto Bethlehem, and see this thing which is come to pass, which the Lord hath made known unto us. And they came with haste, and found Mary, and Joseph, and the babe lying in a manger. . . . And the shepherds returned, glorifying and praising God for all the things that they had heard and seen, as it was told unto them.

—Luke 2:1, 4–16, 20

Now when Jesus was born in Bethlehem of Judaea in the days of Herod the king, behold, there came wise men from the east to Jerusalem, Saying, Where is he that is born King of the Jews? for we have seen his star in the east, and are come to worship him. . . . And, lo, the star, which they saw in the east, went before them, till it came and stood over where the young child was. When they saw the star, they rejoiced with exceeding great joy. And when they were come into the house, they saw the young child with Mary his mother, and fell down, and worshipped him: and when they had opened their treasures, they presented unto him gifts; gold, and frankincense and myrrh.

— Matthew 2:1–2, 9b–11